A Note to Parents and Caregivers:

Read-it! Readers are for children who are just starting on the amazing road to reading. These beautiful books support both the acquisition of reading skills and the love of books.

 The PURPLE LEVEL presents basic topics and objects using high frequency words and simple language patterns.

 The RED LEVEL presents familiar topics using common words and repeating sentence patterns.

 The BLUE LEVEL presents new ideas using a larger vocabulary and varied sentence structure.

 The YELLOW LEVEL presents more challenging ideas, a broad vocabulary, and wide variety in sentence structure.

 The GREEN LEVEL presents more complex ideas, an extended vocabulary range, and expanded language structures.

 The ORANGE LEVEL presents a wide range of ideas and concepts using challenging vocabulary and complex language structures.

When sharing a book with your child, read in short stretches, pausing often to talk about the pictures. Have your child turn the pages and point to the pictures and familiar words. And be sure to reread favorite stories or parts of stories.

There is no right or wrong way to share books with children. Find time to read with your child, and pass on the legacy of literacy.

Adria F. Klein, Ph.D.
Professor Emeritus
California State University
San Bernardino, California

Editor: Christianne Jones
Designer: Hilary Wacholz
Page Production: Melissa Kes
Art Director: Nathan Gassman
The illustrations in this book were created digitally.

Picture Window Books
151 Good Counsel Drive
P.O. Box 669
Mankato, MN 56002-0669
877-845-8392
www.picturewindowbooks.com

Printed in the United States of America.

 All books published by Picture Window Books
are manufactured with paper containing at least
10 percent post-consumer waste.

Library of Congress Cataloging-in-Publication Data
Meister, Cari.
Bug race! / by Cari Meister ; illustrated by Burak Senturk.
p. cm. — (Read-it! readers)
ISBN 978-1-4048-4746-0 (library binding)
[1. Stories in rhyme. 2. Insects—Fiction. 3. Racing—Fiction.] I. Senturk,
Burak, 1973- ill. II. Title.
PZ8.3.M5514Bg 2008
[E]—dc22
                                            2008006311

Bug Race!

by Cari Meister
illustrated by Burak Senturk

Special thanks to our reading adviser:

Adria F. Klein, Ph.D.
Professor Emeritus, California State University
San Bernardino, California

PICTURE WINDOW BOOKS
Minneapolis, Minnesota

Calling all beetles! Calling all flies!

4

Let's get ready to exercise!

Welcome all kinds! Welcome all sorts!
Welcome any bug in shorts!

Ready. Set. Go!

The honeybee is fast. The silkworm is slow.

Watch out, everyone! It's quite a show!

The ladybug lost its wing. The cricket stopped to sing.

The firefly took a break to dance. The stinkbug lost his fancy pants!

The damselfly stopped to cry. The june bug ate some yummy pie.

The earthworm could not see. He bumped into the bumblebee!

13

The earwig stopped to lay some eggs. The millipede tripped and lost three legs!

The mosquito stung the ref. The gypsy moth flew too far left.

The caterpillar got stuck in the mud. The tick stopped to drink some blood.

The cicada was too busy whining. The termite was too busy dining.

"Who's left?" cried the judges. "Who's left in the race?"

Which of the bugs will get first place?

The cockroach is looking fine. Perhaps he'll cross the finish line.

But wait! What do we spy? The dragonfly is whizzing by!

Goodness gracious! It's a tie!

More *Read-it!* Readers

Bright pictures and fun stories help you practice your reading skills. Look for more books at your level.

Benny and the Birthday Gift
The Best Lunch
The Boy Who Loved Trains
Car Shopping
Clinks the Robot
Firefly Summer
The Flying Fish
Gabe's Grocery List
Loop, Swoop, and Pull!
Patrick's Super Socks
Paulette's Friend

Pony Party
Princess Bella's Birthday Cake
The Princesses' Lucky Day
Rudy Helps Out
The Sand Witch
Say "Cheese"!
The Snow Dance
The Ticket
Tuckerbean at Big Bone Bowl
Tuckerbean at Waggle World
Tuckerbean in the Kitchen
Wyatt and the Duck

On the Web

FactHound offers a safe, fun way to find Web sites related to topics in this book. All of the sites on FactHound have been researched by our staff.

1. Visit *www.facthound.com*

2. Type in this special code:
   1404847464

3. Click on the FETCH IT button.

Your trusty FactHound will fetch the best sites for you!
A complete list of *Read-it!* Readers is available on our Web site:
www.picturewindowbooks.com